MORDICAI GERSTEIN

Queen Esther
the Morning Star

SIMON & SCHUSTER BOOKS FOR YOUNG READERS

SIMON & SCHUSTER BOOKS FOR YOUNG READERS
An imprint of Simon & Schuster Children's Publishing Division
1230 Avenue of the Americas, New York, New York 10020

Book design by Lily Malcom
The text of this book is set in Elysium.
The illustrations are rendered in Guache.
Printed in Hong Kong
10 9 8 7 6 5 4 3 2 1

Library of Congress Cataloging-in-Publication Data
Gerstein, Mordicai.
Queen Esther the morning star : the story of Purim / Mordicai Gerstein.
p.   cm.
Summary: Retells the story of how a beautiful Jewish girl
became the Queen of Persia and saved her people from
death at the hands of the evil Haman.
ISBN 0-689-81372-4
1. Esther, Queen of Persia—Juvenile literature.
2. Bible stories, English—O. T. Esther. [1. Esther, Queen of Persia.
2. Bible stories—O. T. 3. Purim.] I. Title.
BS580.E8G47 2000
222'.909505—dc21
97-29653
CIP   AC

For
my grandfather Mordecai,
whom I never knew,
and for all the other
Mordecais and Esthers
everywhere

Author's Note

Legend has it that the reason the heroine of this story was named
Esther, which means Venus, the morning star, is because hers
is the last book of the Old Testament, and Venus is the last to
fade after all the other stars are gone.
I've found several meanings for Mordecai, from "messenger of God,"
to "excellent myrrh." Both Esther and Mordecai are
Babylonian names, and come from the time
Jews were exiled in Babylon.
Because Mordecai is my namesake, and my grandfather's (and
maybe even my great-grandfather's), Purim, the Jewish holiday
that celebrates Mordecai and Esther, has always had special meaning
for me. It was also a lot of fun!
As children we went to temple dressed as characters from the story,
and whenever Haman's name was mentioned in the service, we
booed and whirled our noisemakers, called "groggers." And of
course we stuffed ourselves with the pastries called
"hamantashen." Before eating the first one, we always liked to
say, "Thank you, Haman!" I liked the prune kind best.

It is told that King Ahasuerus of Persia, whose
kingdom stretched thousands of leagues from India
to Ethiopia, gave a great banquet for all the princes,
governors, and satraps over whom he ruled. The
banquet lasted for six months. Each day
one hundred different delicacies were served on
golden plates that were used only once and thrown away.
"Am I not the richest of kings?" Ahasuerus asked his guests.
"And is not my queen the most beautiful of all queens?"
"You are the richest of kings," agreed all the princes,
governors, and satraps, "but we have not seen your queen.
Where is she?"
And so the king summoned Queen Vashti to
come and display her beauty.

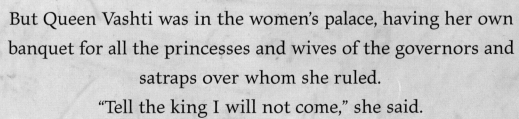

But Queen Vashti was in the women's palace, having her own
banquet for all the princesses and wives of the governors and
satraps over whom she ruled.
"Tell the king I will not come," she said.

"Won't come!" roared the king. "I'll teach her!
Guards! Throw her out! Let her beg in the streets!
I will find a new, *more* beautiful queen. One that *obeys* me!"
And the king commanded that all the beautiful young women
of his kingdom be brought to the palace so he might
choose the *most* beautiful.

Out of all the beautiful young women of his kingdom,
one seemed to shine and leave the others in darkness.
Her name was Esther, which means morning star.
"My new queen," the king announced, "shall be Esther."

Now, Esther lived in the care of her cousin Mordecai who,
when her parents died, had raised her as his own daughter.
"Dear cousin," Esther said, weeping, "I don't want to be queen
and live apart from you. No man may visit me except the king,
and I fear him."

"He can be foolish," said Mordecai, "and cruel. Be careful. Do
not tell him who your family is, or that you are a Jew. There are
those at court who hate our people. But know that every day
I shall wait at the palace gates for news of you."

And one day, as Mordecai waited and worried at the palace
gates, Haman, the king's prime minister, came by.
Haman was an evil schemer. He'd coaxed the king to order
everyone to bow down to him.
But Mordecai did not bow down.
"Who are you that will not bow to me?" snarled Haman.
"I am Mordecai, a Jew. I bow only to God."
"I'll have you *hung*!" raged Haman. "And *all* your people, too!"

That night Mordecai dreamed of darkness, thunder, and screams. And out of the darkness two roaring dragons rose up to battle each other. People cried for help and their cries became the stars in the sky. Then the morning star blazed and the sun rose. The innocent were saved and the wicked were destroyed.

Mordecai awoke. "What is the meaning of this dream?" he wondered. It was exactly midnight.

At that same moment Haman was saying to the king,
"Your Majesty, there is a people who have strange customs
and obey only their own laws. They scorn you and your rule.
They are dangerous and you must rid your kingdom of them."
"What people are these?" said the king with a yawn,
for it was past his bedtime.
"The Jews," said Haman.

"I'm tired," said the king. "Do with these Jews as you wish."
And he went to sleep.
But gleeful Haman and his wife stayed up all night casting lots,
called "pur," for the date when the Jews would be destroyed.
And the lot fell on the thirteenth day of the twelfth month—
Adar, in the Hebrew calendar.

Then Haman sent letters to all the princes, governors, and
satraps from India to Ethiopia, which said: "On the thirteenth day
of Adar, all the Jews—young and old, men, women, and children—
are to be killed. Seize their possessions and send them to me."
He sealed the letters with the king's ring.

When they learned of Haman's letter, all the Jews in Persia,
from India to Ethiopia, put on sackcloth and ashes and
wept and wailed.

And Mordecai at the palace gates did the same.
Then he understood his dream.
"The two dragons stood for Haman and me," he realized.
"And the morning star was Esther. She must save our people!
I must get a message to her."

"I will take your message," said a voice.
It was Queen Esther's servant (though some say it was the
angel Michael in disguise).
"Tell the queen," said Mordecai, "that she must tell the king
she is a Jew and plead with him to save her people from Haman."

And Esther sent back a message that said: "Tell my cousin that the king has not called for me in thirty days. And if anyone, servant or queen, comes to the king without being called, she is put to death, unless he raises his golden scepter."

"Tell my dearest queen," said Mordecai in return, "that she must take the risk, or all of us —young and old, men, women, and children—shall be put to death."

"When Esther heard this, she put on the most beautiful robes, jewels, and perfumes the king had given her and went to see him without being called.

"Who comes uninvited?" he thundered. "Do you wish to die?"

But when he turned and saw Esther,
he was overcome with love.
"Whatever you wish," he said, raising his golden scepter,
"even half my kingdom, is yours."
"I wish only," said Esther, "to beg . . ."
"Yes?" said Haman, who had just come in. "What is it?"
"To beg . . ." stammered Esther, thinking quickly, ". . . that you
both come to a banquet I will prepare for you tomorrow."
A banquet! thought Haman. *The queen must favor me!*

That evening Haman started home happily,
until he met Mordecai at the gate.
"You and your people are doomed, Jew," sneered Haman.
"Bow down!"
"Never," said Mordecai.
Haman arrived home, his eyes popping with rage.
"I am prime minister of Persia," he screeched to his wife, "and
all the lands from India to Ethiopia! I dine with the king
and queen! But that Jew, Mordecai, won't bow to me!"

"Why wait to kill Mordecai?" said Haman's wife. "Build a
gallows tonight and tell the king to hang him in the morning."
"Brilliant!" cried Haman, happy again.
"I'll make it fifty cubits high!"
And Haman and his ten sons set to work building the gallows
where Mordecai would hang.

But meanwhile, after Haman had left him at the gate, Mordecai
heard whispering in the bushes. It was the king's cook
and butler plotting to kill the king.
"Tonight I'll poison the king's soup," said the cook.
"And I'll serve it to him!" said the butler. "Death to the tyrant!"

Immediately, Mordecai wrote a
note and gave it to the guard.
"Take this to the king," he said.
"It will save his life."

The king was lifting a spoonful of soup to his lips when the guard gave him the note. It said:
"Your Highness:
Don't eat the soup. It has been poisoned by the cook and butler.
Your faithful subject, Mordecai."

The king called the cook and butler and ordered them to taste the soup. They trembled and refused.
"TASTE IT!" shouted the king.
They did, and both fell over dead.
"Call the prime minister," the king ordered.

When the gallows were finished, Haman rushed to the king to arrange Mordecai's hanging. But first the king asked him, "How should I reward someone who has done me the greatest service anyone can do?"

"Why, Your Majesty," replied Haman, sure the king meant him, "you should dress him in your own robes, give him ten thousand pieces of silver and gold, and have him led through the city on your finest horse in a great parade."

"Excellent!" cried the king. "You yourself may bring Mordecai here, and you may lead his horse in the parade!"

Haman almost swallowed his false teeth.

"Do you mean Mordecai the Jew?" he croaked.

"If that's what he is," said the king, "that's who I mean. He saved my life."

And so all was done as Haman had suggested. He muttered curses as, instead of hanging Mordecai, he led him on the king's stallion through streets of cheering people.

Even being a guest at the queen's banquet later didn't cheer
Haman up. "Ask for the stars," the king said to Esther,
"and they shall be yours."
"I ask, sire, only that you answer one question:
What would you do to someone that planned the death of me
and all my people?"
"Why, I would hang that person!" said the king.
"From a gallows fifty cubits high!"

"Your prime minister, Haman, sire, is that person.
For I am a Jew and so is my cousin Mordecai.
And on the thirteenth day of the twelfth month,
Haman has ordered the death of all Jews."
"Why, so he has!" said the king. "I completely forgot!
I don't even remember why he wanted to do such a
stupid thing. Guards," he cried, "take him away!"

Haman was hung on his
own gallows the very
next day.

Mordecai became prime minister and went to live in the palace,
where he could be close to his dear cousin Esther.
And on the thirteenth day of the month of Adar, all the Jews
had a great celebration.
And to this day, they still do.
It is called "Purim," after the lots Haman cast.
Everyone laughs, dances, makes noise,
and tells the story of Esther and Mordecai.

And all that remains of Haman is his name,
as part of the word *hamantashen*, a delicious pastry
shaped like his hat.
And for that, we may thank him.